Other books by Karen Katz

Mommy Hugs

Ten Tiny Tickles

Daddy Hugs 1 2 3

Counting Christmas

Counting Kisses

Twelve Hats for Lena

Margaret K. McElderry Books

Margaret K. McElderry Books

An imprint of Simon & Schuster Children's Publishing Division

1230 Avenue of the Americas, New York, New York 10020

Copyright © 2008 by Karen Katz

Book design by Ann Bobco

The text for this book is set in Bookman Oldstyle.

The illustrations for this book are rendered in gouache, colored pencil, and collage.

Manufactured in China.

10 9 8 7 6 5 4 3

Library of Congress Cataloging-in-Publication Data

Katz, Karen.

Ten tiny babies / Karen Katz.—1st ed.

p. cm.

Summary: Babies from one to ten enjoy a bouncy, noisy, jiggly day until they are finally fast asleep at night.

ISBN 978-1-4814-0132-6

[1. Babies—Fiction. 2. Counting. 3. Stories in rhyme.] I. Title.

PZ8.3.K1283Te 2008

[E]—dc22

2007036061

0217 SCP

ten tiny babies

by karen katz

Margaret K. McElderry Books
New York • London • Toronto • Sydney

To
Ann B., Karen W., Baby L.,
and all the little cuties
in the world.

1 tiny baby starts to run.

Along
comes
another...

...to

have

some

fun.

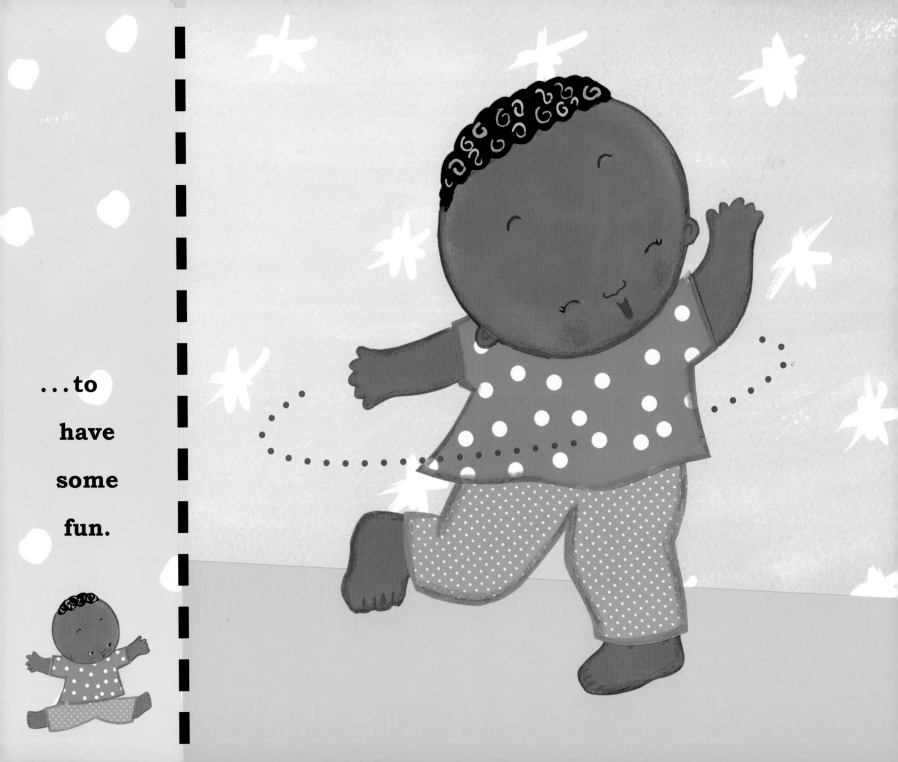

2
silly
babies
spin
around.

Along comes another . . .

3 bouncy babies

. . . and

she

falls

down.

jump and . . . hop!

Along
comes
another . . .

4 noisy babies

...but he just can't stop!

bang and shout!

Along
comes
another...

. . . to
sing
right
out!

5 jiggly

babies wriggle their toes.

Along
comes
another...

6 hungry babies

. . . who

wiggles

her

nose!

sip and chew.

Along
comes
another...

7 dirty babies

. . . she'll nibble some too!

scrub-a-dub.

Along
comes
another . . .

8 cuddly babies

...straight

into

the tub.

put their pj's on.

Along comes another...

9 drowsy babies

. . . with a big, sleepy yawn.

crawl to bed.

Along comes another...

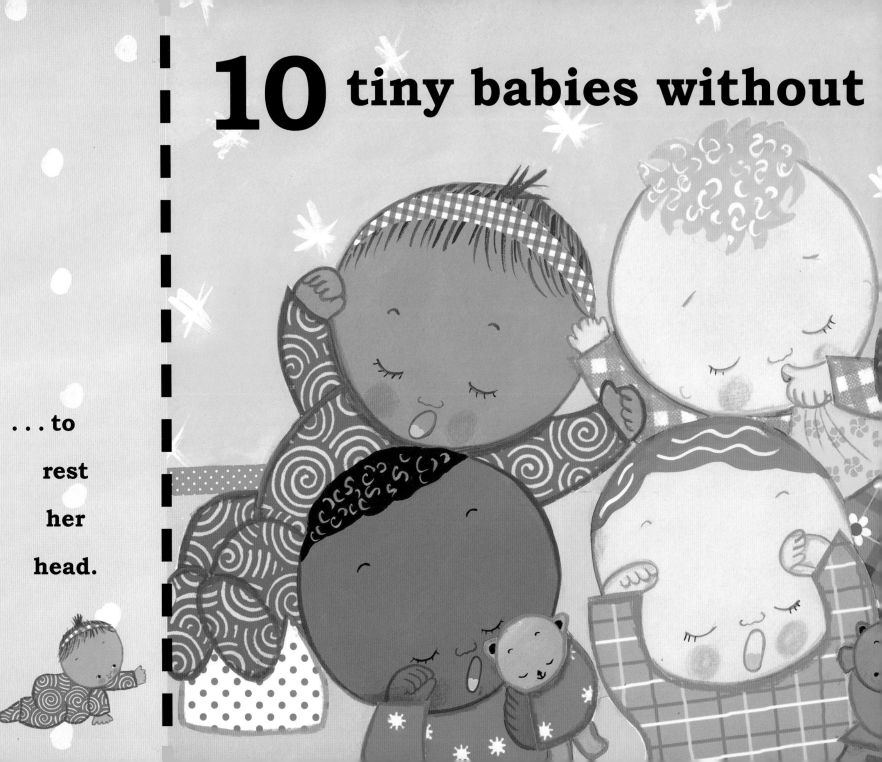

10 tiny babies without

. . . to rest her head.

a peep. . . .

babies are fast asleep!

Good night, babies!